CROWBAR

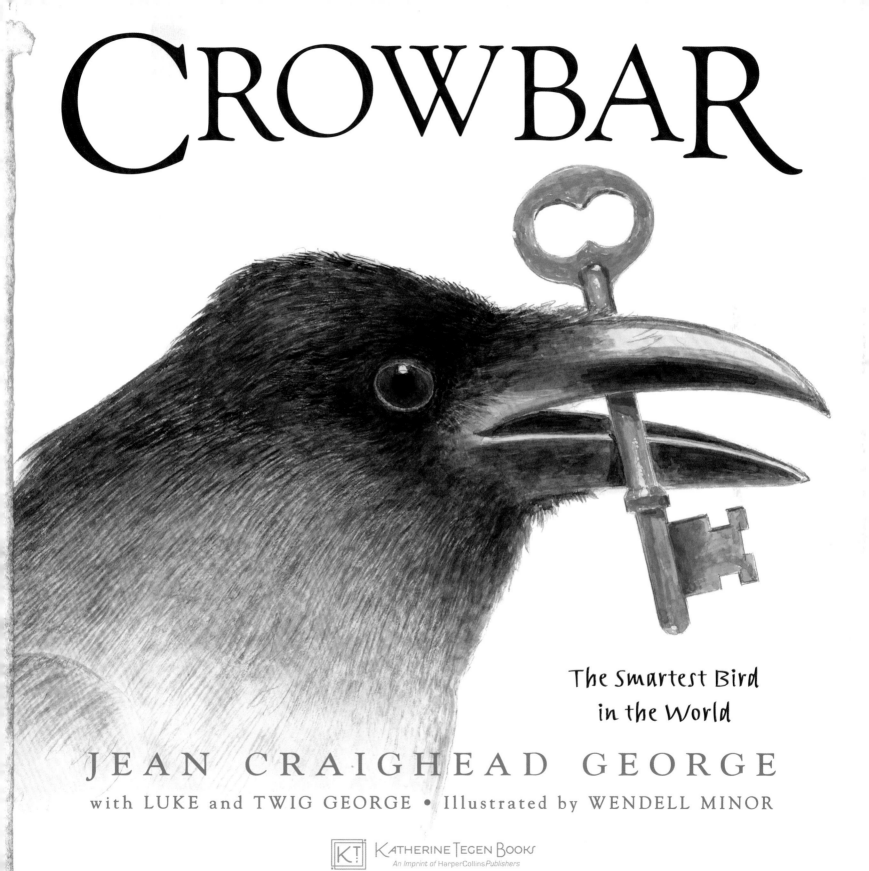

The Smartest Bird
in the World

JEAN CRAIGHEAD GEORGE

with LUKE and TWIG GEORGE • Illustrated by WENDELL MINOR

KT KATHERINE TEGEN BOOKS
An Imprint of HarperCollins Publishers

On a walk early one spring morning, I spotted a baby crow on the ground. He was too young to fly, and he was wobbly and cold. Two cats watched hungrily. I knew he wouldn't last long. I couldn't find the nest or his parents, so I tucked him under my shirt and carried him home.

As soon as I got home, my mom showed me what to do. I fed the baby crow hamburger and cheese until he fell asleep in my arms. "Can we keep him?" I asked.

Mom paused. "It's a hard job," she said softly.

She worked at a bird rescue center, helping injured and orphaned birds, so she knew not all of them made it.

"Please, Mom?" I begged, and held my breath.

"Okay. You can keep him, but only until he's ready to live on his own. And he's very weak. He may not live very long."

"I know," I said sadly, "but we can try."

"I'd be careful if I were you. Crows can be real pests," Grandpa called from the next room.

"Crows are smart! And his name is Crowbar," I answered.

"A crowbar is a tool, not a bird." Grandpa was getting a little testy.

"Crows use tools. And he's only mine for a little while."

"Only humans use tools," said Grandpa.

I knew it wasn't true, but how could I prove it to Grandpa?

I made Crowbar a bed in a box. A short time later,
Crowbar made raspy cries. "He thinks you're his mother,"
Mom said. "He needs to be fed." I fed him thirty times a day.

Crows are scavengers. They can eat anything, so I fed him
hamburger, cheese, eggs, and even chunks of corn muffins.
He ate and ate and ate! How did his parents find enough
food with no hands or grocery stores?

In a few days, he could stand.

In two weeks, he was bouncing out of his box.

In a month, Crowbar was able to fly.

"He eats. He calls. He flies! When are you going to let him go?" grumbled Grandpa.

Almost as if he understood what Grandpa had said, Crowbar walked to the open door. He fluttered his wings and flew outside.

But . . . Crowbar didn't fly away. Instead, he took up a perch in the apple tree near the kitchen window. Our yard was now his home!

Crowbar lived outside and learned to eat beetles, frogs, and worms, but he was still part of our family. He rapped on my window every morning and cried, "Caw, caw, caw," to wake me up. I opened the window and let him in.

At breakfast, he ate my leftovers. His favorite was bacon and eggs.

On school days he walked beside me to the bus stop. He sat on
the fence with us until the bus came.

Mom said when the bus was gone, he flew home and cawed four
times at the kitchen window. She knew then I was off to school.
Grandpa watched and didn't say a word.

Mom gave me a book about bird communication.
I learned that crows speak to each other in their own
language. Their words are

"caaw"

and "ta-ta-ta-to"

and "dong."

I heard Crowbar practicing outside.

"Because you're part of Crowbar's family," Mom explained, "he'll learn the words you say if you repeat them often enough, like a parrot."

I said hello enough times to teach a salamander. But Crowbar would not speak English.

Grandpa watched and didn't say a word.

One day our mailman knocked on the door. He looked surprised
when I opened it. "I swear I heard you say hello from that tree," he said.
    I ran across the yard.

    "Hello!" I heard my own voice coming from high in the apple tree.
Crowbar flew down to my shoulder.
    "Hello," he repeated.
    "Mom, Grandpa," I yelled. "Come out here. Crowbar can speak!"
Mom flung open the door.
    "Hello," Crowbar said to her.
    "Now, that's really smart," I said.
    Grandpa didn't say a word.

Crowbar learned how to use his words to his advantage. He would fly to our neighbors' picnics, land on the table, and say, "Hello!" in a clear voice. Worried, the neighbors would herd their children and friends inside away from this strange, talking crow. He would gobble down their potato salad, hamburgers, hot dogs, cheese, and olives. Then, just like a wild crow, he would hide some tidbits in a tree!

When my mother heard there was a talking crow that invaded picnics, she laughed. "He won't hurt anyone," she told them. "He just wants a treat."

Soon Crowbar was a welcome guest at local picnics.

If he was smart enough to join picnics and hide food, I hoped he could learn to be a wild crow.

One day, Mom's new bracelet disappeared.

"I bet Crowbar hid it," I said. Sure enough, I found it in the
sugar bowl. "Crowbar's smart. He seems to know what we think
is important."

Grandpa grumbled something about pests.

Next, I couldn't find my lunch money.

"Maybe Crowbar likes money, too," Grandpa said.

"Or he knows we like it." I said, "And that's really, really smart."

We found my money in the flowerpot.

"But that's not a tool," Grandpa mumbled as I took my money
and left for the school bus with Crowbar right behind me.

My friend Melissa came over one day. We made
a city in the sandbox and used Mom's best spoons
as flags for the castle. Crowbar flew down to join us.
Suddenly he snatched a spoon and flew off with it.

"Mom," I called, "I'm not playing
with that crow anymore. He steals!"
"Told you; crows are thieves!"
Grandpa cackled.

"Well, play on the slide," Mom suggested from the doorway. "Crows can't slide. Their feet are designed to hold on to tree limbs without slipping."

Melissa and I chased each other down the slide. Once, twice, three times.
Grandpa came out to watch.
Crowbar flew to the top of the slide, landed, and fluttered his wings.
He didn't move an inch.
"You showed him!" Grandpa shouted.

With that, Crowbar flew to the sandbox and picked up a jar lid he liked to play with. He carried it to the top of the slide and stepped on it.

ZOOM! Down the slide went Crowbar.

Grandpa shouted to my mother, "Come out here and see this. That dang crow just used a tool!" He turned to me and said with a smile, "Look at that—crows are pretty darned smart!"

"Really smart," echoed Melissa.

Over the next few weeks, Crowbar spent less and less time with us. I missed him. One day, a great flock of crows landed in the yard. I looked at each bird, but I couldn't tell if Crowbar was among them. Then one bird dropped out of the tree, cocked his head, and cawed four times. It was Crowbar!

I didn't know it then, but he was saying goodbye.

The next time the cloud of crows lifted, Crowbar was gone.
He had joined his flock. They would teach him the rest of
what it was to be a crow.
I was sad but proud; my job was done.

FIND OUT MORE ABOUT CROWS

• **Could I have a pet crow?**

The main character in the story could keep Crowbar because his mother had a wildlife rehabilitation license. Also, the baby crow was in danger of being eaten by cats. If you find a young bird that cannot fly, you should always try putting the bird in a safe spot off the ground (a bush or a tree) and let the parents continue feeding it unless it is in imminent danger.

If you find a bird that cannot fly and cannot be left where you found it, you should put the bird in a dark box and contact a local wildlife rehabilitation center. There are wildlife rehabilitation centers in many towns and most large cities in the US. For information about rehabilitation centers near you go to:

www.humanesociety.org/resources/how-find-wildlife-rehabilitator

The Migratory Bird Treaty Act prohibits the possession of wild birds except for those individuals with a valid rehabilitation permit or to transport an orphaned or injured bird to a rehabilitation center. For more information go to:

www.fws.gov/permits

- **Watch a crow sliding down a roof like Crowbar!**
  On YouTube search for: Crow Uses Plastic Lid to Sled Down Roof Over and Over Again

- **Watch a New Caledonian crow not only use a tool but modify it to make it work better:**
  On National Geographic search for: Tool-Making Crows Are Even Smarter Than We Thought

- **New Caledonian crows are really smart. Watch this bird solve an eight-part puzzle!**
  On YouTube search for: Crow Solves An 8 Step Puzzle To Get Food

- **Watch this to understand more about the calls of crows and ravens:**
  On YouTube search for: Caw vs. Croak: Inside the Calls of Crows and Ravens

- **Do you know what a group of crows is called?**
  A murder of crows!

BACKGROUND INFORMATION
FOR TEACHERS AND PARENTS

Check out these books about the intelligence of crows and other birds:

Ackerman, Jennifer. *The Genius of Birds*. New York, Penguin Press: 2016.

Marzluf, John, and Tony Angell. *Gifts of the Crow: How Perception, Emotion, and Thought Allow Smart Birds to Behave Like Humans*. New York: Free Press, 2012.

Yolen, Jane. *Crow Not Crow*. Cornell Lab Publishing Group, 2018.

Katherine Tegen Books is an imprint of HarperCollins Publishers.

Crowbar: The Smartest Bird in the World
Text copyright © 2021 by Julie Productions, Inc.
Illustrations copyright © 2021 by Wendell Minor
All rights reserved. Manufactured in Italy.
No part of this book may be used or reproduced in any manner whatsoever without written permission except in the case of
brief quotations embodied in critical articles and reviews. For information address HarperCollins Children's Books, a division of
HarperCollins Publishers, 195 Broadway, New York, NY 10007.
www.harpercollinschildrens.com

ISBN 978-0-06-000257-2

The art in this book was created using graphite and Designers Gouache on Strathmore 500 Bristol and digitally enhanced.
Typography by Caitlin Stamper
21 22 23 24 25 RTLO 10 9 8 7 6 5 4 3 2 1
❖
First Edition